The Three Musketeers

A long time ago, in a beautiful part of France called Gascony, where people were known for their hot tempers and their courage, there lived a young man named d'Artagnan. His greatest dream was to become a musketeer—one of the very special guards of the king of France.

One day, d'Artagnan's father presented him with a letter and said, "Son, the time has come for you to make your fortune in Paris. Take this letter to Monsieur de Tréville. He is a fellow Gascon and captain of the king's musketeers. He will help you." Then, he added, "Listen carefully, for what I am about to tell you is of utmost importance: always defend your honor, and always be determined and courageous."

Eager to embark on his new life, d'Artagnan set off for Paris on the old family horse. The horse made a very loyal companion, but also a funny-looking one, since it happened to be covered in spots.

En route to Paris, d'Artagnan came to the town of Meung, where he crossed paths with a nobleman and his lackeys.

"Ha! Will you look at that horse?" said the haughty nobleman, "I have never seen such a ridiculous sight! It is covered in spots!"

Chuckling, one of his lackeys replied, "Why with all those spots, it looks more like a cow than a horse!"

And with that, all the men laughed loudly at d'Artagnan and his horse.

Remembering his father's words, d'Artagnan bravely declared, "Here in my hand is a very important letter of introduction that will permit me to become a musketeer! Neither I, nor my horse, will be mocked by the likes of you!" Singling out the nobleman, he added, "I demand an apology, or we will face off in a duel!"

The men laughed even harder, and shoved d'Artagnan. When he tried to fight back, he lost his balance and fell into a deep mud puddle. The men continued to laugh uproariously as they left the scene.

After d'Artagnan managed to get up and clean off as best he could, he realized that the nasty nobleman had stolen his precious letter!

Armed with the determination that his father had spoken of, d'Artagnan continued his journey. He no longer had the letter, but he still had his dream of becoming a musketeer!

When at last d'Artagnan arrived in Paris, he wasted no time in calling on Monsieur de Tréville, and requesting an audience with him.

Monsieur de Tréville's impressive antechamber was filled with musketeers waiting for their turns to meet with him. As d'Artagnan looked about in awe, a loud voice suddenly announced, "D'Artagnan! Monsieur de Tréville will see you now!"

When he entered Monsieur de Tréville's chamber, d'Artagnan noticed the captain was in a foul mood. Before even greeting d'Artagnan, Monsieur de Tréville called for three of his musketeers: Athos, Porthos and Aramis.

However, only Porthos and Aramis appeared, explaining that Athos had been seriously injured in a fight the night before.

Looking very annoyed, Monsieur de Tréville, said to both of them, "I know of the disturbance you caused last night. As the king's musketeers you cannot go about picking fights, resisting arrest, and sword fighting! There is a law against dueling!"

Then, having expressed his displeasure, Monsieur de Tréville dismissed the musketeers.

Alone with Monsieur de Tréville, d'Artagnan introduced himself. He told him of his wish to become a musketeer, and all about his unpleasant encounter with the nobleman in Meung who had stolen his letter of introduction.

Impressed by his fellow Gascon's sense of honor, courage, and determination, Monsieur de Tréville offered to write d'Artagnan a new letter recommending him to the Royal Academy so that he could pursue his dream of becoming a musketeer!

As Monsieur de Tréville was penning the letter, d'Artagnan looked out the window, and quite unbelievably saw the mysterious nobleman from Meung! Without waiting for his new letter, he bolted after him!

While in pursuit of the man, hotheaded d'Artagnan accidentally plowed into Athos, the musketeer who had been injured in the previous night's fight. Furious with d'Artagnan for hurting his already injured shoulder, he challenged him to a duel at twelve o'clock.

D'Artagnan accepted the challenge.

14

D'Artagnan then resumed his chase, this time running head-on into pompous Porthos, and accidentally exposing that Porthos' belt buckle only had gold on one side, instead of on both! Embarrassed, Porthos challenged d'Artagnan to a duel at one o'clock.

D'Artagnan accepted the challenge.

Again, d'Artagnan tried to resume his pursuit of the mysterious man from Meung. As he looked around, he saw Aramis, who, chatting with some nobles, was unaware that he was standing on a lady's handkerchief.

D'Artagnan picked up the handkerchief and handed it to Aramis, who then accused him of having been rude for drawing attention to the matter. He then challenged d'Artagnan to a duel at two o'clock.

For a third time, d'Artagnan accepted the challenge!

Now faced with the prospect of three duels in a row against excellent swordsmen, d'Artagnan realized that his chances of winning were not very good! Worried, yet determined, he courageously headed off to confront his opponents.

When d'Artagnan arrived at the agreed upon location, Athos was already there waiting for him, and was soon joined by Porthos and Aramis.

D'Artagnan got into position, and Athos did the same. Just as the duel was about to begin, the men were unexpectedly interrupted by a troop of the cardinal's guards.

With their swords drawn, and ready to fight, the cardinal's guards rushed onto the scene, declaring, "Stop at once! There is a law against dueling! You are all under arrest!"

But the musketeers would not allow the cardinal's guards to arrest them, and the guards would not back down! D'Artagnan had a decision to make: would he fight on the side of the cardinal's guards, or would he side with the king's musketeers? Without hesitating d'Artagnan joined the ranks of the musketeers!

A spirited sword fight ensued, with d'Artagnan using excellent sword technique and his best maneuvers. Thanks to him, the king's musketeers soundly defeated the cardinal's guards.

The musketeers were not only thankful for d'Artagnan's loyalty, but also impressed by his skillful fighting. They now had a great respect for this young hot-tempered and courageous Gascon, and welcomed him into their fold, making him the unofficial fourth musketeer!

When the king heard of this latest brawl, he was not pleased. However, he was curious to know more about this man named d'Artagnan who had helped defeat the cardinal's guard. So, the king called for a meeting with him. Although the king could not approve of reckless dueling, he was still very interested in recruiting the best swordsmen for his guard!

When d'Artagnan met with the king, he described the battle against the cardinal's guard in great detail. Impressed, the king rewarded d'Artagnan with a large sum of money. D'Artagnan, in a gesture of camaraderie with the Three Musketeers, shared the king's reward with them.

D'Artagnan was overjoyed at having met the king and at having earned the respect and friendship of the Three Musketeers. He was now well on this way to becoming a real Musketeer of the Guard, and hoped to one day cross paths again with the mysterious man from Meung!

"All for one, and one for all!"